W9-AST-381

Blue Eyes Better

RUTH WALLACE-BRODEUR

PUFFIN BOOKS

PUFFIN BOOKS
Published by the Penguin Group
Penguin Putnam Books for Young Readers,
345 Hudson Street, New York, New York 10014, U.S.A.
Penguin Books Ltd, 80 Strand, London WC2R ORL, England
Penguin Books Australia Ltd, 250 Camberwell Road, Camberwell, Victoria 3124, Australia
Penguin Books Canada Ltd, 10 Alcorn Avenue, Toronto, Ontario, Canada M4V 3B2
Penguin Books (N.Z.) Ltd, 182-190 Wairau Road, Auckland 10, New Zealand

Penguin Books Ltd, Registered Offices: Harmondsworth, Middlesex, England

First published in the United States of America by Dutton Children's Books,
a division of Penguin Putnam Books for Young Readers, 2002
Published by Puffin Books, a division of Penguin Putnam Books for Young Readers, 2003

1 3 5 7 9 10 8 6 4 2

Copyright © Ruth Wallace-Brodeur, 2002
All rights reserved

CIP Data is available.

Puffin Books ISBN 0-14-250086-0

Printed in the United States of America

Except in the United States of America, this book is sold subject to the condition that
it shall not, by way of trade or otherwise, be lent, re-sold, hired out, or otherwise
circulated without the publisher's prior consent in any form of binding or cover other
than that in which it is published and without a similar condition including this condition
being imposed on the subsequent purchaser.

OTHER PUFFIN BOOKS YOU MAY ENJOY

Slipping away . . .

When I got home, I pulled a soggy newspaper out from behind the hydrangea bushes and put it in the trash barrel. I chopped some ice in the driveway, and I filled the bird feeder. Then I went inside.

The silence was louder than Scott's music had ever been.

"Mom?" I called. There was no answer. "Mom?" I hung up my jacket and went into the living room. Mom was all curled up in the blue recliner chair. Her eyes were open, but she didn't seem to be looking at anything. She still had on her bathrobe.

I stood right in front of her. "Mom?" My voice quavered. I reached out and touched her arm. Then I shook it. "Do you want some tea? Did Mrs. Goldberg come? Do you want me to call her?"

"For heaven's sake, Tessa, stop jarring me!" Mom sat up straight and pulled her robe tight around her. "Yes, I guess I should drink something. . . ." Her eyes were looking at nothing again.

When I brought the tea, she let it get cold on the table beside her.

★ "A fine choice for any[one] coping with grief or a grieving parent, and an exquisite example of spare, honest prose."
—*Publishers Weekly*, starred review

★ "Overall, this is hopeful but unsentimental, an honest chronicle of the kind of experience that isn't real until it happens to you." —*BCCB*, starred review

Donated by the Bensenville Rotary

With love and thanksgiving for Paul

AT MY BROTHER'S FUNERAL, my father's neck above his white collar was as red as the stained-glass window beyond. The window showed Jesus tending a flock of puffy white sheep. I liked seeing through clear glass better.

My father and I stood up for the hymns, but we didn't sing. My mother didn't even stand up. Aunt Rhoda sat with her and handed her tissues. Mom cried most when Angus Stewart played "Amazing Grace" on the bagpipes. I tried to shut my ears and do multiplication tables in my head. Scott used to play that song on his harmonica.

After the service Reverend Leeds came down from the pulpit and shook hands with us and with Gramma and Grampa Drummond. She said she was very sorry about Scott. Then we followed her up the aisle and downstairs, where everybody else was supposed to say they were sorry and eat sandwiches and cake. I went out the fire door into the alley between the church and the back of Wardsboro City Hall. It was Thursday of February vacation week. Scott was killed Monday night at 9:47. That's what his smashed wristwatch said. Aunt Rhoda had given him that watch in December for his sixteenth birthday.

I was already asleep that night, but I woke before the doorbell rang. I heard a man say, "Is this the Drummond residence?" Then my mother cried "No!" and I knew without anybody saying one more thing that Scott was dead. My mother kept screaming "No!", so I didn't hear what my father and the policeman said. My father came up and listened at my door, but I didn't move. Then they all went off and it was quiet. I wasn't usually left alone that late at night, but it was okay. I was going to be eleven in July. If anything happened while they were gone, I could call the Goldbergs. I could go out my window onto the porch roof and climb down the cedar tree and run over to their house. It's the next street over. Hannah Goldberg's been my best friend since our first day at kindergarten.

When my parents got back, my father came and stood at my door again. "Tessa?" he said real soft, but I didn't answer. I didn't want to know any more.

I don't think my parents went to bed at all. They had on the same clothes when I went downstairs in the morning. People I never saw before were there, and the phone kept ringing. I sat at the kitchen table. I can get my own breakfast, but I wasn't hungry. When my father came, I said "I know" before he could tell me. He told me anyway. He said that Scott had been riding with Kevin Olsen. He said Kevin had been drinking and maybe thought he could beat the train that hit them.

Scott had told my parents he was going to the movies with Grady Allen, but I knew he was meeting Kevin Olsen at the corner. I heard him tell Grady on the telephone. He said Grady could come, too, but Grady didn't like Kevin. Scott was going to take driver education after February vacation. He wasn't supposed to ride with other kids, especially not

Kevin Olsen, but he did, and I knew it. Now he was dead, and so was Kevin.

I came out of the alley onto Vine Street. It was gray and cold. I pulled up my kneesocks and began to walk home. The socks slipped down with every step. I'd put on a dress to please Mom, but she hadn't noticed. She hadn't noticed much of anything since Monday.

When I got to my street, I kept walking. I didn't want to go home. I wished I could go to the Goldbergs', but they were in Florida. Their plane had left Logan Airport at 6:30 Tuesday morning. They probably didn't even know Scott was dead.

Aunt Rhoda had come Tuesday morning and was staying until Sunday. She tiptoed around, making herbal tea and ordering cartons of rice and vegetables from Ling Mai's. She said rice and vegetables were good for times of stress. The white boxes were stacked in our refrigerator like snow blocks in an igloo.

Gramma and Grampa Drummond had come out from Boston in their Buick Tuesday and Wednesday, but they wouldn't eat any of the Chinese food. They just sat on the sofa and sighed. Gramma wanted me to sit next to her. She wiped her eyes and blew her nose on a little handkerchief she stuck up her sleeve. "You're the only one now," she whispered in my ear. She got me all damp. Grampa shook his head and said, "No one left to carry on the family name." I told him I intended to be Tessa Drummond my entire life, but he kept saying it anyway. My mother and Aunt Rhoda call Gramma and Grampa "The Taps." It means Those Awful People, but I'm not supposed to know that.

The streets near where we live are lined up like the steps of a ladder between Ralston Street and Boylston. I walked along one and back the next until I got to the rotary by the highway. It was getting dark, so I walked straight back Ralston to my street, Oak Street. Hannah lives on Pine Street. All the streets on the ladder are names of trees.

Cars were parked in our yard and along the curb. The Smollens from across the street were just leaving. An eyelash moon gleamed in the sky above their house. After all that had happened, there it was. I watched it brighten, then I went up our driveway and through the kitchen door. Gramma's pink baking dish was on the counter. It smelled like fishy tuna casserole. My father hates tuna casserole. He said that in all his years of growing up, that's all his mother ever cooked.

I hung my coat on one of the pegs by the door. Scott's maroon Wardsboro High jacket fell off the next peg. It made me cry the way the sleeve curled around my ankle. My tears plopped on the nylon.

I tried to get past the living-room door and upstairs without anyone noticing, but Dad was watching for me. He came and stood at the foot of the stairs.

"I was worried," he said. "I looked everywhere." His eyes were darker than usual. They are hazel, the same color as mine. Scott's were light blue, like my mother's.

"I went for a walk," I said. He nodded and held out his hand. I went back down to him and put my head against his chest. He wrapped his arms around me and held me until Gramma and Grampa came into the hall.

"We'd best be getting back, Ed." Gramma waited for Dad to find her coat and help her into it. "You tell Shirley to buck up," she said as she pulled on her fake-leopard hat and gloves. "She's got another one needs looking after." She looked at me with her sad-dog eyes. "Poor lamb. Give Gramma a kiss." I tried to turn my cheek, but she smacked her wet lips right on my mouth.

"No one to carry on the family name now." Grampa shook Dad's hand. He took out his wallet and thumbed through the bills. "You get yourself a little treat," he said as he folded my hand around five dollars.

Dad stared at the door after they'd gone. "Everything changes and it's all the same," he said. "Try to eat something, Tessa. And let your mother know you're back."

Mom wasn't with the people downstairs. I found her sitting on the edge of her bed. "Please turn up the heat" was all she said when she saw me. "It's cold in here."

THE NEXT MORNING I dialed Hannah's number over and over. I listened to it ring in their empty kitchen, then hung up before the answering machine came on. "Hi, it's me" would be all I could say. Even in my mind I couldn't get out "Scott is dead."

Hannah had always thought Scott was a big deal. Maybe it was because she was an only child. Scott never paid much attention to her. He didn't pay much attention to me, either. I asked Mom once why he didn't like me. She said he loved me very much, it's just he was so much older and had other interests. But Trudy Arvid's brother was older than Scott, and he paid attention to her. He picked her up after school, and he took her to movies and ball games. If anybody acted like a big brother to me, it was Grady. He was the one who always said "Let her come" when I asked to go with him and Scott to the Tastee-Freez. He was the one who used to hold my hand crossing Boylston Street.

Aunt Rhoda came downstairs with a tray from Mom's room. "Tessa honey," she said. "Stop fiddling with the phone. I need to call my shop." Even in February, Aunt Rhoda smelled like mowed grass. She told me it was an expensive perfume called Summer Song. She put the tray in the kitchen, then went into Mom's office. She closed the door, but I could still hear.

"Karen?" she said. "Thank God you're there." It was the first time I'd heard her normal voice all week.

I thought maybe it would be a good time to try to see my mother. I went up and knocked on her door. She didn't answer, so I opened it just a crack and peeked in. She was sitting in the rocker by the window.

"Can I come in?" I asked. Her door was hardly ever shut.

"Of course," she said. She didn't look at me.

I sat on the bed. "Do you want me to get you something?" I asked after a while.

"No, thank you. I'll be down in a bit." She sounded polite. Like she was talking to someone she didn't know very well. I couldn't see her face because of her hair. She usually tied it back. It was curly and bright brown, like Scott's. The color of an autumn leaf, my father said. Mine is straight and plain dark brown.

"I could brush your hair," I offered. Mom always loved that.

She sighed and said in that polite voice, "Go find your father, Tessa. Maybe he'll take you to the aquarium or something."

She was trying to get rid of me. She didn't want to see me, she didn't want to talk to me. I tiptoed out and shut the door without a sound.

I lay on my bed and looked at the jungle I'd painted on my walls. My tears made the river look real. The head and back of a rhinoceros stuck up out of the water in the section by my bed. An elephant was hosing its baby next to my desk, and a giraffe bent down to get a drink between the bureau and the door. Scott had said I was ruining the house when I started painting, but sometimes he looked in to see if I'd added anything.

I didn't want to paint it anymore. All I wanted was to be with my mother, but she didn't want to be with me. I couldn't think of a single thing to do. My father was working in the cellar, and Hannah was gone. I couldn't just call up somebody else at a time like this.

I wiped my eyes and looked at the clock by my bed. At 1:30 I could pick up the *Wardsboro Wise* and do my Friday route.

I got my jacket and my newspaper bag and went to sit on the cellar stairs. A fire was snapping in the woodstove behind Dad's bench. Dad was gluing one of the kitchen chairs.

My father is older than most of my friends' fathers. His hair is all gray. He told me his hair went gray years ago when he was a pilot in the Vietnam War. He said that after that war he wasn't fit for much of anything. He waited a long time before he married my mother. My father is fifty-seven and my mother is fifty-one. They thought Scott would be their only child. I was a surprise. A wonderful surprise, my father said.

Dad looked up at me as he tightened a clamp. "When will the Goldbergs be back?"

"Sunday," I said. I watched the wood pull together. "Late Sunday."

He nodded at the bag in my lap. "You intend doing your route?"

"It's Friday," I said. "I can go early because of no school."

"Scott was lucky he had you for a sister." My dad bent over the chair again. All I could see was the top of his head. I wanted to grab on to his thick hair, the way I used to when I was little and he carried me on his shoulders. I wanted him to tell me exactly why he thought Scott was lucky to have me for a sister.

Was it because of the paper route? I'd started doing it the week before Thanksgiving after Scott had one of his asthma attacks. I promised, "Please, God, let him breathe and I'll do his paper route." It was the only thing I could think of at the time, and it worked.

Scott hated doing the route right from the start.

He took it because he wanted more money. Mom wanted to raise his allowance, but Dad said no, he'd have to earn it. Dad hardly ever disagreed with Mom and held firm, which was probably why he didn't want to let me do the route.

"I think Scott should quit complaining and stick to his commitment," he'd said when I asked.

"It's not his idea," I said. "I just really want a paper route. Scott's almost sixteen. He can find a job he likes better. *Please,* Dad."

In the end, Dad agreed. From the quiet way he'd looked at me, I think he knew there was more to it than I was saying. But a promise to God is like a birthday wish. You can't tell it, and you sure don't want to break it.

"You're nuts," Scott said when I told him I would do the route. "Don't ask me to substitute."

I never asked anybody to substitute. I liked the route and I liked the money. The *Wardsboro Wise* covered local news and shopping. It came out once a week. All I had to do was put the paper on every porch for five streets, including my own.

I watched Dad work until it was time to go. He didn't talk anymore, but the way he looked up at me every now and then, I could tell he liked me being there. I felt better by the time I left.

A fine snow was falling, just enough for my sneakers to leave tracks on the sidewalk. I ran all the way to Hal's Mobil station, on Ralston Street, where the papers were dropped off. Hal came over and helped me fill my bag. He didn't say anything about Scott, which I thought was very nice.

"You're looking a mite chilled" was all he said when I came back for a second load. He gave me cocoa in a mug that had a picture of the Bunker Hill Monument on it and said BEANTOWN, USA.

I could see Mrs. Hirsch watching for me in her window. From the first time I'd met her on my route, I knew she was the kind of person I would choose for a gramma. Today I pulled my hood way up and pretended I couldn't hear when she knocked on the glass. I felt bad doing that, but I didn't feel like smiling and waving like nothing had happened, and I wasn't ready for a visit. When I finished the route, I went home the long way, through the park and all around the rec field. The snow was falling faster. My feet scuffed fans in it.

Dad would be gone when I got back. He was sup-

posed to meet with some insurance ዞ
dered if he'd still think Scott was luck
for a sister if I told him I'd known Sc
to ride with Kevin Monday night. Maybe I'd tell
him sometime. I could never tell Mom. Not ever.

"Promise you'll call if you need me," Aunt Rhoda said when she was all set to go on Sunday. We still needed her then, but I could tell she was glad to be leaving.

I almost choked on the urge to yell "Wait for me!" when her car slowed before turning on to Ralston Street. Aunt Rhoda lives in an old house in Truro on Cape Cod that belongs to her and my mother. I love it almost more than our house in Wardsboro. Even in winter it smells like blueberry bushes and pine needles and ocean. My mother's parents and grandparents lived there. They all died before I was born.

Not before Scott was, though. Our albums have twenty-four pages of pictures of Scott with his Ahmy and Pops. That's what he called my mother's parents. Pops had a heart attack when Scott was three, and Ahmy died a year later. I wish they'd been my Ahmy and Pops, too.

Mom went back to her bedroom as soon as Aunt Rhoda left. Dad and I made a big pot of spaghetti sauce, then we watched a program about polar bears and part of a basketball game. The day, like all the others since Monday, seemed endless.

Mom didn't eat any of the spaghetti for supper, but she sat with us and drank tea.

"Am I supposed to go to school tomorrow?" I asked.

Mom looked straight at me for what seemed like the first time since Scott died. The crinkles around her eyes were flattened out. It made her look different. She reached out a hand and tucked my hair behind my ear. "Do you feel up to it?" she asked.

"Yes. No. I don't know." I wanted to say whatever would keep her looking at me.

"Do you want me to stay with you?" I asked. Dad had been going to stay home another week, but

Mom didn't want him to. She said she thought work was the best thing for him to do.

"No. I won't be needing anything." Mom held her teacup against her chest and bent her face over it. I couldn't tell if she was crying again or trying to get warm. Dad pulled a chair up close to hers and stroked her hair. I cleared the table and started the dishes. She'd gone back upstairs by the time I finished.

The next morning Dad had my oatmeal ready when I came down. Dad and I were the only ones who ate oatmeal. Scott said it was disgusting. He said oatmeal was for peasants. Mom usually had toast and coffee for breakfast.

Dad used to work in an office, but he got migraines, so he left to drive a truck for Pure Sass Organic Sauces. He liked the people and the driving and not having to get dressed up. He was wearing the purple plaid flannel shirt I picked out for him at Christmas.

"Come right home from school," he said when he was getting ready to go. "I don't want your mother to be alone all day."

I nodded. "Is she going to get up?"

"I don't know. She will soon, Tessa. We have to

give her time." He kissed the top of my head. "I'll be home by six. We'll heat up that spaghetti."

I washed the bowls and the oatmeal pot, then I went upstairs and stood outside my mother's door. The hall was dark, with my mother's and Scott's doors shut all the time.

"Mom?" I said. "I'm going to school now."

There was no answer. I went back downstairs and wrote a note.

Dear Mom,
   I had breakfast and washed the dishes. I will come right home from school. I hope you feel better. I love you.

                        Your loving daughter,
                              Tessa
P.S. I will vacuum the living room when I get home.

I WAS SURPRISED to see it was sunny outside. I breathed in so hard the cold air hurt my chest and made my eyes water. It was early. Maybe Hannah wouldn't be at the corner yet. Maybe she got home too late to go to school today. Maybe she didn't get home at all. I decided not to look until I got to the first telephone pole.

She wasn't there, and then she was. I started to run. Instead of waiting for me to get to the corner, Hannah ran toward me. We stood there, hugging and crying.

"I just found out, Tessa," Hannah said when she could talk. "I didn't think you'd come. I was going to go to your house, but I didn't know if you'd want me to."

"I called you all week," I said. "Even though I knew you weren't there."

Hannah dried her face on her turtleneck, but the tears kept coming. "Are you sure you want to go to school?" she asked. "I'll stay home with you."

I shook my head. "It's okay. My mother wants me to go."

"My mom's baking bread for her," Hannah said. "She's going to bring it sometime today."

"Good." My mother liked Mrs. Goldberg. She was a social worker at WomenCenter on Maple Street. Maybe she would know what to do.

We didn't talk on the way to school. We walked so close our jackets made kissing sounds.

As we got near the school, I wasn't sure I wanted

to go in. What if I started to cry again? I tried a deep breath. Things seemed drier inside. I sure didn't want to spend another day at home.

Hannah was watching me. "Are you nervous?"

I took another breath. "I guess it will be okay. Just don't cry again, Hannah, and don't watch me funny."

"I won't," Hannah promised. "Here." She took a wooden dolphin barrette out of her pocket and gave it to me. "I've got a pelican one."

Our classroom got quiet when we walked in. I went to my desk and took out my math book. I could tell everyone was looking at me. I started to trace the dolphin on the back cover and hoped Mr. Gomez would begin very soon. I heard him clear his throat.

"Tessa," he said. I didn't look up from my dolphin. "We are very sorry. If you need to leave at any time, you go right ahead. You may go with her, Hannah. Now, everybody turn to page eighty-seven and let's see if that section is still causing trouble."

I did okay. Trudy Arvid passed me an orange candy heart that said *My friend* on it. It tasted like licorice. Emma Washburn wove me a necklace of gum wrappers during silent reading, and Adam Kestler put a Scripto pen on my desk when we went to lunch. I figured know-it-all Walter Plum would have a lot to say about Kevin's drinking, and maybe about Scott, too, but he didn't. Hannah told me later she said she'd jam his brains down his throat if he said one word about anything.

The hard part was when we went to music. Ms. Dunn was everybody's favorite teacher even on her quiet days. She was tall and had long red hair and the only really green eyes I'd ever seen. Brittany Bevins said she dyed her hair, but I didn't care if she did or not. She wore a tiny silver flying bird pin in a different place every day. Sometimes we had to look a long time to find it. When she first came to our school, she wanted everybody to call her Abby, but Mrs. O'Leary, our principal, said we had to call her Miss Dunn.

"Better make it *Ms.* if you want me to answer," Ms. Dunn told us. Brittany said a lot of people called her Will-Be Dunn, but after a while even Brittany and Mrs. O'Leary said *Ms.*

The walls of the music room were covered with painted masks that Ms. Dunn got in Mexico. We'd made colored mobiles to hang from the ceiling that were codes for different chord patterns. Music was always playing except when we sang or played instruments ourselves.

As soon as I got in the room, I could feel something inside start to crumble. "I have to go to the bathroom," I said, and I left real fast.

Ms. Dunn wasn't supposed to leave the class unattended, but she did. She came right after me into the washroom. I was standing around the corner by the sink. I was shaking so hard my teeth chattered. Ms. Dunn wrapped me up against her. "It's the music, Tessa," she said. She rocked me back and forth. "It won't let you hide when your heart is breaking. Do you need to go home?"

I shook my head. "My father's at work," I whispered.

"What about your mother?"

"I don't want to upset her."

Ms. Dunn kept rocking me. "Music will help you, Tessa, but not right now, not in class. I'll give you assignments in the library until you feel you're ready to come back." She held me until I calmed down, then she went with me to the library and found me a chair by myself in the sun. She told the aide I would be coming in three times a week to read about composers.

"What happened in music?" Hannah asked when

we were walking home. "Ms. Dunn said you'd be doing research in the library for a while."

"I can't listen to music right now," I said. "It makes me feel bad."

"Oh." Hannah was quiet beside me. "I thought everything would make you feel bad. I thought you wouldn't be able to go to school for feeling bad."

"No," I said. "My mother cries all the time, but not me."

"What about your dad?"

"He tries to help my mom."

"Ms. Dunn is the best," Hannah said after a while. "Do you want to come over?"

"I can't," I said. "I'm supposed to go straight home."

I watched her walk away from me when we got to the corner of my street. "Call me!" I yelled. She turned and waved. Maybe tomorrow I could go to her house. We always went to my house or hers after school. Hannah probably wouldn't come to mine until my mother felt a little better.

When I got home, I pulled a soggy newspaper out from behind the hydrangea bushes and put it in the trash barrel. I chopped some ice in the driveway, and I filled the bird feeder. Then I went inside.

The silence was louder than Scott's music had ever been.

"Mom?" I called. There was no answer. "Mom?" I hung up my jacket and went into the living room. Mom was all curled up in the blue recliner chair. Her eyes were open, but she didn't seem to be looking at anything. She still had on her bathrobe.

I stood right in front of her. "Mom?" My voice quavered. I reached out and touched her arm. Then I shook it. "Do you want some tea? Did Mrs. Goldberg come? Do you want me to call her?"

"For heaven's sake, Tessa, stop jarring me!" Mom sat up straight and pulled her robe tight around her. "Yes, I guess I should drink something. Jane brought some bread this morning, but I wasn't up for much of a visit. How did you manage in school?"

"Okay," I said. "Everybody was watching me, but they didn't say anything." I didn't tell her about music.

"You'll probably need to talk about this at some point."

She didn't mean then. Her eyes were looking at nothing again. When I brought the tea, she let it get cold on the table beside her.

On the first day of spring, Adam Kestler put a daffodil on my desk. Nobody saw him do it, but I knew because he was careful not to look at me all morning. Plus Walter Plum said Adam's mother was selling daffodils for the Cancer Society that day. Mr. Gomez got me an empty milk carton to put it in until I went home.

Real spring took a long time coming. I was waiting for it, thinking maybe my mother would feel better when the forsythia bloomed. She always put branches of it in the blue Chinese vase in the hall. But a big snowstorm came the first of April. When the forsythia finally did bloom under the dining-room windows, I was the only one who noticed. I put some in the blue vase and in every other jar and vase I could find, but it wasn't the same as Mom doing it.

We didn't do anything for Easter, either. Reverend Leeds visited my mother the day after and brought her a lily from church. Mom said it reminded her of Gramma Drummond and put it out on the kitchen steps.

I did get to celebrate Passover, though my parents didn't go. We always went to Hannah's house for Seder. The Goldbergs invited lots of people. We said the same prayers and ate the same food every year. Mr. Goldberg always told the story of the Jewish people passing from slavery in Egypt to freedom. This year Mrs. Goldberg talked about how hard times can lead to good changes. I was glad to hear that. Then she played the piano and people sang and some danced.

The first really warm day didn't come until the Friday after Seder. It was cold and raining when I went to school in the morning, but warm and sunny when I came out. All of a sudden, trees and bushes were lacy green, and I could smell the earth. Hannah had to go to her piano lesson, so I ran all the way home.

"Hi, Mom," I yelled when I came in the door. She was in her office, working at her computer. I thought that was a good sign. Mom's an accountant. She's really good with numbers. She can figure things in her head faster than you can get the answer on a calculator, and she remembers any date or telephone number she's ever heard. She hadn't worked much since Scott died.

"Do you want me to open the windows?" I asked. "It's really nice out."

She turned and looked at me with her ironed flat eyes. "Sue Allen came by," she said. "They're dedicating today's opening game to Scott. She wanted to know if I'd like to go with her."

"Are you going to?" But I figured she wasn't even before she shook her head. She hadn't even opened the door to Scott's room yet.

"I saw the team practicing," I said. "Grady's playing second base this year."

"Yes." Mom took my hand and started pushing the cuticles back on my fingernails. "Sue said he didn't want to catch for anyone after Scott. She said he feels responsible."

"What for?" I didn't like having my cuticles pushed back, but I didn't want to take my hand away.

"Because he said no when Scott asked him to go that night."

"If he went he might have been killed, too," I said.

"He thinks maybe he could have talked Scott out of going when they saw Kevin had beer in the car."

"What did you say?"

"I said that's something we'll never know."

I took my hand away. "I'm going to do my route," I said, and went to get the bag.

"Wear your jacket," she called as I ran out through the kitchen, but I didn't. If she opened a window, she'd know I didn't need a jacket.

I was still running when I cut around the corner of Hal's Mobil station and crashed straight into Ms. Dunn. We grabbed each other to keep from falling. "Whoa!" she said. "Hit by a shooting star!" She held me at arm's length. "How are you, sweetheart? Kicking up your heels on this gorgeous day?"

I'd never seen Ms. Dunn outside of school. She had on jeans and an olive shirt that made her eyes look even greener. She'd been putting air in her bicycle tires.

"I like to run," I said.

She gave me a hug before letting go. "Good," she

said as she finished putting the air hose back on the pump. "Because I'm coaching summer track at the rec field this year. Think you'd be interested?"

I nodded. I was good at running. I'd won the four-hundred-meter race last year at field days by a lot.

"Well, that's terrific," Ms. Dunn said. "Let your friends know. It starts the week after school lets out."

She blew me a kiss as she rode off. I hadn't told her we went to Truro in the summer. Maybe we wouldn't go this year. Everything else was different.

"We finally got a lemonade day," Hal said when I came in. He took a carton from the cooler, stuck a straw in it, and handed it to me. He shook his head as he watched me stuff papers into the bag. "That's too heavy for a little girl like you." He said that every week.

"Thanks for the lemonade." I managed to squeeze out through the door without spilling any.

Halfway down Walnut Street, Mr. Doyle was pushing his lime spreader back and forth on his lawn. It looked like the only yard that still had snow. His shoes were all white, too.

He stopped when he saw me putting my lemonade

carton in his trash can. "Hello there, young lady. And what did you learn this week?"

Mr. Doyle was bald except for a ruffly white fringe that looked like a halo. He shuffled when he walked. He'd told me he had the sugar and couldn't feel his feet. He worked in his yard whenever it was nice out, and he always asked what I had learned in school. If I remembered, I tried to have something ready to tell him.

"I learned that cedar waxwings are called waxwings because they have a splotch of red on their wing feathers that looks like sealing wax," I said.

"Now, there's a bird for you," Mr. Doyle said as he stuck the paper in his back waistband. "They act as pretty as they look. Did you know they're one of the few birds to feed each other? I've seen it myself, right in that cranberry bush there. You tell that to your class. It's worth knowing."

"I will." I was glad it was warm enough for Mr. Doyle to be out now.

Mrs. Hirsch was out, too, rocking on her porch for the first time that spring. "Come sit awhile," she said when I handed her the paper. "I look for you every Friday, but you hurry by. I worry for you, such a terrible thing."

I sat down in the green wooden rocker next to hers and took a gingersnap from the plate she passed.

"I'm okay," I said.

"Yah, life goes on for ones left behind, though when my Ira died I don't see how it could. I tell the sun not to come. I like the rain better. At least it take notice."

"I like the sun," I said. "I've been waiting and waiting for it."

"You are young." Mrs. Hirsch passed me more cookies. "And thin, Tessa, too thin. You eat." She tipped the rest of the gingersnaps into my lap. "Maybe sometime I tell you about my Ira, and you tell me about your brother. You cry and I cry and then we have cookies." Mrs. Hirsch nodded and rocked and ate another gingersnap. I finished the ones she dumped in my lap and rocked myself up.

"See you next week," I said. "Thanks for the cookies."

"You come in if I'm not out here," she called after me. I waved and nodded. I'd been noticing that lots of people who seemed perfectly normal had had someone die on them.

My last street was Maple Street. A gray striped cat lived in a purple house with raspberry trim. I called her Clementine because she had big double paws. I sat on the raspberry steps and waited. Pretty soon she came out from under the porch and jumped into my lap. "I wish you were my cat," I said as I rubbed her ears. Clementine purred and nudged my chin with her nose. I couldn't have pets because Scott and my mother were allergic.

Clementine walked with me to WomenCenter on the corner. I watched her go from bush to tree back to her house. Then I crossed Boylston Street to the rec field.

I stood behind the fence by third base. Todd Walbridge was pitching. The green scoreboard above the snack shack said it was the last inning. Wardsboro was ahead 3-2, but Southfield had two on base and no outs. Todd walked the bases full, then let one across on a wild pitch. Grady fumbled a ball at second that should have set up a double play, and two more runs scored. Southfield won, 5-3.

Scott hadn't been good at most sports, but he could pitch. Nobody minded that he couldn't hit or field because his pitching was so good. Mom went to every single game, home and away. She and Mrs. Allen took turns driving to the away games. Dad was usually working, but he went to all Scott's summer league games. Mom said baseball was good for Scott's confidence. I thought he had plenty of confidence, but maybe there are different kinds.

Dad was making vegetable lasagna and Mom was washing asparagus when I got home. They hadn't cooked together in a long time. Dad bent down to hug me when I leaned against him. I held on to his neck when he straightened and wrapped my legs around his waist the way I used to when I was little.

My mother whacked the asparagus against the edge of the sink to break off the tough ends. "Aren't you getting too big for that?" she asked.

"Never," Dad said. He tightened his arm around me and layered the last of the lasagna noodles with one hand.

"Tastee-Freez is open," he said when we'd finished eating. "Anyone interested?"

I looked at Mom. She loved going to Tastee-Freez as much as I did. We were always excited when it first opened for the season.

Mom shook her head. "I'm not up for it," she said. "Maybe another night."

"How about you, Tessa?" But Dad wasn't smiling anymore, and I didn't want to go anyway.

"No, thank you," I said. "I think I'll paint on my wall."

I put some new trees in the jungle, then lay on my bed. Before Scott died, Mom would never have said I was getting too old to be held. She wouldn't have said what she did to Mrs. Allen, either. She would have told her what happened wasn't Grady's fault. Because it wasn't. Scott knew Kevin drank. Everybody knew it. If Grady had said something, maybe Scott wouldn't have been his best friend anymore. Scott hadn't been very nice to leave Grady for Kevin anyway. Scott could be a real jerk sometimes. I was tired of thinking about him.

MOM LEFT US IN MAY. She told us two days before she went.

"Just for a week," she said. "I want to supervise putting Scott's headstone in the cemetery in Truro. And Rhoda could use a little help getting the shop ready. Provincetown seems to have more tourists and less help every year.

"I'm not doing either of you any good here," she went on when neither Dad nor I said anything. "Tessa feels she has to keep her eye on me, and you haven't even started your garden, Ed. With me gone, maybe you'll get on with your lives."

"You seem to have this all arranged," Dad said.

Mom frowned, and her nostrils widened the way they do when she's angry.

"For heaven's sake, Ed, it's just for a week. You and Tessa can come Memorial Day weekend to see the stone and pick me up."

"Thank you," Dad said. "I would like to have some part in that."

They stared at each other, then Mom turned to me. "I've talked to Mrs. Goldberg, Tessa. You can go there after school until your father gets home."

I just nodded. I could hardly breathe.

Mom left early Saturday morning with the Smollens. They were going to their cottage near Truro for the weekend. I watched to see if Mom and Dad kissed good-bye. They didn't, but Mr. Smollen was showing Dad his new animal radar when Mom got in the car, so they didn't really have a chance.

"Well," Dad said when the car had turned the corner, "I guess it's you and me, Tessa."

I took his hand. "It'll be okay, Dad," I said.

He looked down at me and smiled. He traced my nose with his thumb. "Did I ever tell you," he said, "about the time I was holding you up to see a beautiful rainbow, and gold dust puffed up from the pot at the end of it and showered down on you? And that's how you got your freckles? Did I ever tell you that?"

"I think I remember," I said. The way I always did.

We spent the day getting seeds and plants for the garden and putting up poles for the beans and a fence for the peas. That night Dad read to me from a book about a man who made a boat out of animal skins and followed a route a monk named Brendan took hundreds of years ago. It was really good.

Sunday morning I went over to Hannah's while Dad played racquetball at the gym. I'd already had breakfast, but Mr. Goldberg had made waffles, so I had some of those, too. I noticed he kissed the top of Mrs. Goldberg's head when he put waffles on her plate. She smiled at him and touched his hand.

It was raining, so after Hannah and I helped clean up the kitchen, we went up to her room to braid friendship bracelets.

"Do you mind that your mom went?" Hannah asked when we were sorting the embroidery thread.

I shrugged. "I don't know. I guess she wants to talk to Aunt Rhoda. Maybe she'll get warmed up and keep talking when she gets home. She doesn't say much to me or Dad."

"That's because she's so sad," Hannah said. "Sad people don't have much to say."

"She always had a lot to say to Scott. If I had died instead of Scott, I think she'd talk to him. She said they were kindred spirits."

"What does that mean?"

"It means she liked him in a special way. Like they were sort of the same, you know? She says I'm all Drummond."

"Well, she likes your dad."

"She doesn't like his parents. And neither do I."

"You're not anything like them," Hannah said. "And your mother likes you."

I concentrated on my braiding. After a while I said, "She likes blue eyes better than mine."

"How do you know that?"

"Because she was always buying Scott clothes to match his eyes and telling him how good he looked. Nothing matches my eyes."

Hannah studied me. "I like how you look," she said. "Your eyes are all different colors. Sort of like a kaleidoscope. My mom says you stand out."

"Really? Is that good?" It wasn't the same as pretty or beautiful, but I did like kaleidoscopes.

"It's the best," Hannah said.

"Do you think your mother told mine that? About me standing out?"

Hannah nodded. "Probably. They talk about us all the time."

"Not anymore." I sighed. "She probably forgot." I looked at how Hannah's hair curled down from her pelican barrette. "Maybe I'll get one of those hair-wave things in a box. Maybe we could do it before my mother comes back and surprise her."

"It wouldn't be true," Hannah said. "And it stinks. My mother did it once, and we had to open all the windows and turn on the fan. She didn't like how it came out. That's the time she cut her hair real short."

I measured my bracelet on Hannah's wrist. "Let's wear these even in the shower, Hannah. Let's never take them off." We braided them extra long in case they shrank. I tied mine on Hannah's wrist and she tied hers on mine.

Gramma and Grampa Drummond were sitting on the sofa when I went home. I could tell Dad wasn't very happy to see them. It had stopped raining and he wanted to work in his garden, but they thought it was too cold to sit outside. Gramma said a week was too long for Mom to be leaving us. Grampa said Scott was a Drummond and his stone should be with the Drummonds in Lexington. Dad got pretty quiet and I pretended I had to read the Brendan book for homework. By the time they left, it was too late for Dad to garden, so he just watched TV.

I went home with Hannah after school every day that week. In the evenings after supper, Dad and I got most of the garden planted. Dad made the rows and I put the seeds in. On Saturday we were going to Truro for Memorial Day weekend and to get Mom. Friday was my last chance to do something I wanted to do when nobody was home.

I told Mrs. Goldberg I'd be late getting to their house because of my paper route. Then I did the route as fast as I could. Mr. Doyle and Mrs. Hirsch just waved. They could see I was in a hurry. When I finished Maple Street I ran home, got the key from under the kitchen steps, and let myself in.

The house was quiet, but not a loud quiet like when Mom was there. The refrigerator was humming and the clock ticked at the end of the hall. Dad had opened the door to Scott's room, which made the upstairs brighter.

Scott's clothes were still in his closet. His stuff was on his desk and shelves. Everything was neatened up, though, not like when he was alive. His harmon-ica was in its box on the bureau. His inhaler was on the table by his bed. Computer books and programs were lined up in the rack on his desk.

Dad had opened the window as well as the door. I wondered if he would shut them again before Mom came home. I sat on the bed in the sun and looked at the Red Sox poster on the wall. A picture of Scott with Roger Clemens was next to it. It had been taken before Scott got tall.

My father was tall and my mother was tall and I'd always been one of the tallest kids in my class. Scott used to be the shortest in his. It bothered him more than anything. My mother worried it was maybe be-cause of the asthma, but Aunt Rhoda said no, she had asthma and she was big and strong as a horse. Dad was so afraid it might have been something he'd breathed in Vietnam that I was as happy for him as I was for Scott when Scott started to grow. He grew eight inches from when he was fourteen until he died. He measured himself all the time. The marks were on his closet door.

I lifted the edge of the quilt. Scott's maroon blanket was there, but the sheets were gone. Mom must have taken them off and neatened up his room when she was home by herself.

I got up and opened the closet door. Scott's trumpet case was on the shelf. His ball glove was hanging from a hook on the back of the door. He never kept it there. He always stuck it on his bedpost.

I took the trumpet out and tried to blow it. Scott took lessons and played in the high-school band. At home he mostly played his harmonica, though. When Scott got the trumpet, I wanted an instrument, too, but Mom said to let him have his day in the sun first.

I pushed in among Scott's shirts until I was standing on his baseball cleats. I could smell him in there. Noxzema and old shoes and Mennen Speed Stick. His blue blazer hung flat against the back wall. He wore it when he went to the Christmas ball with Amy Fontaine. It was the first dance he went to. He was a nervous wreck. My mother taught him the box step that afternoon. He said nobody danced like that any-more, but she said it would give him confidence to know the basics.

He was real excited when Amy asked him to go. He liked her for a long time. But then he got nervous. Grady told Scott he had to go even if he had an asthma attack. They were supposed to double-date, and Grady said he wasn't going to go by himself with Nancy Geiger. Scott got Amy a red rose with some holly around it. Grady got the same thing for Nancy, only her rose was white. Mr. Allen took them to the dance, and Dad picked them up.

I sat down on Scott's shoes and leaned back against the wall. I was just breathing his smell. When I came out of the closet, I took his favorite denim shirt and his ball glove with me. I'd liked how Scott looked in that shirt. It did match his eyes.

I hung the shirt in my closet. I put the ball glove on my bedpost. That night when I went to bed, I brought it under the blankets with me.

WE LEFT AT SIX Saturday morning to beat the traffic. Mom came out of the house as soon as we turned in between the hedges. "There's my Tessa," she said as she opened my door. She leaned in and hugged me before I was out of my seat belt. "I missed you," she said into my hair.

She didn't hug and kiss Dad, but she patted his cheek. And she made his favorite bacon and pancakes with strawberry syrup for breakfast.

We went to the cemetery first. Scott's marker was just a flat stone with SCOTT ANDREWS DRUMMOND and the dates he was born and died cut into it. There were five other Andrews stones near his. They belonged to Mom's parents and grandparents and a great-aunt. We planted flowers around them every spring.

There was a big hole dug next to Scott's stone. My parents poured some of his ashes in it from the tin that had been sitting on the bookcase by Mom's desk since Scott died. Then they planted a lilac bush from the hedge by the house on top. The ashes didn't look like the ones from our fireplace. They were lighter colored and coarse like gravel. We had put some under the crabapple tree in our backyard at home, too.

Seeing Scott's name on the stone made me feel kind of like when my first tooth came out. All my life it had been in my mouth. I didn't think about it or even know exactly what it looked like. Then all of a sudden it was outside in my hand. There was just a space left that hurt when I breathed air on it.

The foghorn at Highland Light started after I went to bed that night. It was raining when I woke up in the morning. Mom and Dad went to church while Aunt Rhoda and I worked on a jigsaw puzzle.

"How did you and your dad make out alone all week?" Aunt Rhoda asked. Even though she was still in her green silk robe, she had on eye makeup and bright red lipstick that matched her fingernails.

Aunt Rhoda doesn't look anything like my mother. Her hair is dyed black with silver streaks and cut very short. Her teeth are white and shiny as piano keys. Mom said she'd had them capped one by one as soon as she started earning her own money. She wears little glasses shaped like cats' eyes on the end of her nose. She has six different colors to go with her outfits. Aunt Rhoda's clothes swish, her jewelry jangles, and she laughs and talks loud.

Mom looks quieter, but I think she's very pretty. She can be fancy, too, like when she and Dad go out, or the time she took belly-dancing lessons at WomenCenter. She looked like a gypsy queen then. But mostly she wears ordinary skirts or pants and shirts like Mrs. Goldberg.

I fit the last piece into the border. "We did okay," I said. I didn't want her to think we did too great. She told Mom everything.

Aunt Rhoda leaned back in her chair. "I just don't

want you to take your mom's leaving personally, sweetie. She loves you both very much. Her withdrawal, her anger—it's all part of grieving."

I looked at her. "Dad and I did fine, Aunt Rhoda. It was good Mom came. She seems better."

Mom did seem better. She and Dad brought lobster rolls home for lunch, then we all went to Provincetown. Aunt Rhoda went to her shop, but Mom walked out on the wharf with Dad and me to look at the fishing boats. We held hands, with me in the middle.

"You two make the rounds," she said when we were walking back to Commercial Street, "then come by the shop. There are a couple of return orders I need to straighten out."

Dad and I looked in some of his favorite galleries, then we went to the surplus store. Dad got a flashlight and I got a shell bracelet and an umbrella hat. On our way back to Aunt Rhoda's store, we bought saltwater taffy, molasses and licorice for Dad, mostly chocolate, popcorn, and pistachio for me.

Aunt Rhoda's shop was called Rhoda's Den. It was crowded with tourists, even though summer hadn't really started yet. Aunt Rhoda pulled a lavender sweatshirt over my head when Dad and I came in.

"These are selling like hotcakes," she said. "We've only been open a week and I have to reorder." The sweatshirt had a picture of a pink rhododendron flower on it. That was Aunt Rhoda's trademark. She gave me one to take home to Hannah, too. Besides sweatshirts, her store had things like hats and bags and notepaper and baskets. Lots of things had a rhododendron on them.

Mom was still working in the back office, so Dad and I got pizza for everybody for supper, then went to the arcade to say hello to Angel Cardova. Angel was a man who dressed up like a fancy woman and put on shows. His family owned Pure Sass Organic Sauces. Angel let me try on his wig and gave me a coupon for a free ice cream. He put his hand on Dad's shoulder and said he was very sorry about Scott.

Mom stayed to help Aunt Rhoda close the shop when Dad and I went back to Truro. She didn't come home with us the next day, either.

"I'm sorry," she said when we'd come back from the beach and were having lunch. "I can't go back yet."

"But we came to get you," I said.

"I know." Mom took my hand. She didn't look at Dad. "I will come soon, Tessa. I just can't go back yet. I need more time. Rhoda can use my help, and it takes my mind off things."

She seemed to be waiting for me to say something. Her eyes began to water. "Please, Tessa, try to understand."

"Is it Scott's things?" Dad's voice was very quiet. "Do you want me to take care of them?"

"No!" Mom slapped her hands down on the table so hard the silverware jumped. I stared at my plate. "No," she said more calmly. "Thank you, Ed, but I need to do that. When I'm ready."

"Maybe we need to do it together." Dad pushed back from the table. "Get your things together, Tessa. We should start back."

Neither one of us said anything the whole way back down the Cape. When we crossed the bridge over the canal, it started to rain again. It was still raining when we got home. Dad went out to his garden anyway to pound in tomato stakes.

The front doorbell rang when I was putting my stuff away. It was Adam Kestler.

"Hi," he said. "I got these for you." He handed me one of those long skinny boxes of chocolate-covered peppermint patties. Rain dripped from the brim of his baseball cap. He had a white strip at the back of his neck, like he'd just gotten his hair cut.

"Thank you," I said. I nudged the door open wider. "Do you want one?"

"No thanks," he said. "I have to help my dad clean the garage. The box got wet coming over, but the inside should be okay."

I watched him ride off on his bike. He turned and waved before he got to the corner. I wiped the box dry with my shirt and went into Mom's office to open it. I sat in Mom's chair and ate one whole section. They were very good. Wintergreen, not peppermint, and nice and soft.

There was a picture of Ahmy and Pops above Mom's desk. They were looking right at me and smiling. All of a sudden, I knew what I wanted to do. I put some mints in a sandwich bag and got my rain slicker.

"I'll be right back," I yelled to Dad. He straightened up and looked at me, but I just waved. He probably thought I was going over to Hannah's, but at the corner I turned toward Chestnut Street instead.

Mrs. Hirsch must have seen me coming, because she opened the door before I could knock. "Such a surprise," she said. "I make some tea. Oh, so lovely you come this raining Remembrance Day."

The tea was black and sweet, not like Aunt Rhoda's flower kinds. We ate oatmeal raisin cookies and the wintergreen patties.

"Very good," Mrs. Hirsch said when she tried one. "Not hard like sometimes." She looked at me over the top of her glasses. "Now you tell me why you come not on a paper day."

"I need a grandmother," I said.

Mrs. Hirsch nodded. "Of course you do. Everybody need a *bubbe*."

Bubbe was what Hannah called her grandmother in Florida.

"I have one," I said, "but she's not the right kind."

Mrs. Hirsch tsk-tsked. "Poor woman. God help her. I be your *bubbe*, Tessa. Oh, I be a good *bubbe*." She laughed and wiped her glasses. "God is good. No little ones of my own, and here you are, out of the rain. 'I need a *bubbe*,' you say, just like that."

She put her glasses back on and leaned toward me. "And why is it," she said gently, "you need a *bubbe* today?"

I picked at the edge of a mosquito bite scab on my

leg. "My mother went away for a week, and now she doesn't want to come back."

"Ah." Mrs. Hirsch poured me some more tea. "Just what *bubbe*s are for. Don't you worry, little one. She come back."

"I'm going to visit Mrs. Hirsch some days after school," I told Dad that night. "Will you tell Mrs. Goldberg it's okay?"

"Is she the woman over on Chestnut Street who gives you cookies?" Dad asked.

"Yes," I said. "She's my *bubbe* now."

MOM SAID IT WAS entirely up to me whether or not I came to Truro when school let out. It had never been up to me before. Scott was back and forth after he started summer baseball, Dad came weekends and most of August, but Mom and I spent the summer in Truro. That's how it was.

"You have to decide, Tessa," Mom said when she called the Sunday morning of the last week of school. "Your father and I have to make arrangements for you either way. You're certainly welcome to come here, but you need to understand I'm very busy in the shop."

She could have quit the shop. She'd never worked there other summers.

I made up my mind right then. "I'm staying here with Dad," I said. "I'm going to do summer track with Ms. Dunn." I handed the phone to Dad and slammed out through the screen door. I didn't want to hear one more word from her. I had been thinking I *might* stay in Wardsboro, but if Mom had cared in the least bit, I would have gone to Truro in a second.

Our classroom already looked empty on the last day of school. Everything had been taken off the walls and shelves and packed away. Emma Washington's mother made a cupcake for every kid in our room with our names written in green frosting. While we were eating them, Walter Plum stood up and read a list of summer safety rules he'd clipped from the *Boston Globe*.

Mr. Gomez handed out our class pictures and report cards. "You're a great group of kids," he said. "I feel privileged to have been part of your lives this past year. I hope you are as happy with me as I am with you, because Mrs. Baker is leaving, so I'm going to be your homeroom teacher again next year."

Everybody cheered, me loudest of all. Mrs. Baker

was mean to most kids but disgustingly sweet to anyone who had bad things happen. Every time I passed her in the hall, she blinked her eyes at me and made a sad face.

Hannah and I exchanged pictures on the way home. She studied mine carefully. "You can tell this was taken after Scott died," she said. Even though I was smiling in the picture, I knew what she meant.

"I'm going to give the big one to Mrs. Hirsch," I said.

"Don't your parents want it?" Hannah was still looking from me to my picture.

I frowned and turned my face away. "Dad won't care," I said. "He puts the little one in his wallet." Mom kept the big ones in a folder in her desk, but I figured she wouldn't notice if this year's was missing. Maybe I'd stick a little one in there just in case.

We had a cookout that night at the Goldbergs'.

"I won't hear of it, Ed," Mrs. Goldberg said when Dad tried to talk to her about paying her to keep an eye on me when he was working. "This helps us out, too. Otherwise, we'd have to make arrangements for Hannah when I'm with clients."

The Goldbergs and Dad decided Hannah and I

could stay at her house or go with Mrs. Goldberg to WomenCenter when she was working. We liked going to the Center. It was a big old house with swinging basket chairs on the porch. We could read out there or paint in the art therapy room. If she wasn't busy, Lily Williams let us try her massage oils and look at her acupuncture needles. Aunt Rhoda had gone to Lily Williams for acupuncture when she was visiting us last Christmas. She said a pain she'd had in her shoulder for months just drained right out the end of the needles.

Track was from three to five every afternoon. I loved it from the very first day. Ms. Dunn told us she'd run the eight-hundred and the fifteen-hundred-meter races on her high school track team, and done the triple jump. She'd read a lot of books and watched training films to get ready to coach us. She explained the different events, then she said she wanted us to think about why we were there.

"Having fun and getting some exercise are good reasons in themselves," she said. "If you want to take on some of the events more seriously, I hope I can help you do that."

I wouldn't have said it, but my first reason for

doing track was because of Ms. Dunn. Ever since that day in the washroom, I wanted to be near her. I'd returned to music class the very next week. I liked how she noticed me. She seemed to know how I was feeling without us having to talk about it.

Hannah chose the triple jump and the hundred-meter dash. "They don't look too hard," she told me. "I'm just doing this because of you, Tessa."

I liked the long jump and all the races. But by the end of the first week, I knew the eight-hundred-meter race was the one I wanted to work on.

"I figured you'd like that challenge," Ms. Dunn said when I told her. "I've always thought the eight hundred demanded the finest tuning."

Track only went for six weeks, so I figured I didn't have much time for fine tuning.

"Pacing is everything," Ms. Dunn said. "You can't run flat out for two laps, but there's not much room at this distance to let up. You've got to find your rhythm. You've got to be smart."

"Why do you try so hard?" Hannah asked one day when I collapsed next to her in the shade. "Why don't you just have fun?"

"I am having fun," I said. "I want to do it good."

"But you do." Hannah fanned me with a towel. "You run faster than anybody. It's too hot to keep practicing."

"I want to do better," I said.

Ms. Dunn worked with me a lot. I was nervous the other kids would mind, but Hannah said not to worry, nobody except Trudy Arvid wanted to try that hard. Trudy Arvid was really good at the fifteen hundred. Her brother Rob held the record for that distance at Wardsboro High. Trudy said last year even the coach didn't take summer track seriously. He mostly talked to his girlfriend instead of helping kids the way Ms. Dunn did.

Right from the start we had meets with teams from other towns on Tuesdays and Thursdays. I came in first for the eight-hundred-meter race every meet except one where I fell. My picture was in the newspaper two times. Dad came to every meet. He always stood at the third turn. That was where I needed to start going my hardest on the second lap. I liked that he was there. I could tell he was proud of me.

"You should see her, Shirley," I heard him say to my mother on the telephone. "She's like a gazelle.

Abby Dunn says she's got the heart and the body of a champ."

Nobody had ever said things like that about me before. When I won field days at school, Scott said I'd better watch out or I'd turn into an Amazon. He said nobody liked Amazons.

Mom called us Saturday mornings and Wednesdays after supper. Sometimes she called Dad after I'd gone to bed. Usually I couldn't hear what they talked about then because Dad went in Mom's office and closed the door.

Dad and I were doing fine by ourselves. I got home from track, and he got home from work at almost the same time. If I got home first, I set the table and picked greens from the garden. Most nights we ate at the picnic table in the backyard. After supper we sometimes rode our bikes to Osmer Lake and went swimming. We watched the softball league games at the rec field, and we worked in the garden. We went to Truro for my birthday over the Fourth of July, and that was all.

"Is your mother getting better?" Hannah asked the morning after I got back from the Cape. We were playing slapjack on the steps of WomenCenter.

"I think sometimes she's mad at us," I said.

Hannah looked at me and missed a jack. "Why?"

"Dad was telling her about the Pure Sass picnic, and Mom said she didn't know how we could go on with our lives like nothing happened. We were walking on the beach, and she turned around and went back by herself." I collected the cards and shuffled them. "She doesn't know Dad cries sometimes."

"Do you hear him?" Hannah asked.

"He doesn't cry loud," I said. "I see him sometimes when he thinks I'm not around. I came home from Bubbe's one night, and he was in the garden with his head down on the hoe handle. His shoulders were shaking, so I could tell."

"What did you do?" We weren't playing slapjack anymore.

"I went in the house real quiet. We went for a walk when he was done in the garden, and I held his hand."

Hannah sighed. "I hope everything gets better."

"So do I." Bubbe told me it would. But it was taking a very long time.

AFTER THE FOURTH OF JULY, I ran faster every time Ms. Dunn timed me for the eight hundred. Running the eight hundred was what I liked to do best in the whole world. I didn't think about anything except my hair swinging, and my arms and legs going, and breathing a big clear path inside. "*Your* rhythm, Tessa. *Your* rhythm," Ms. Dunn would shout during a race, and that's what it felt like, a song where everything fit.

At the end of every practice, I ran a few laps with Trudy Arvid. I liked that, too, not going as fast as I could, just nice and steady. Like a horse heading home after a hard day's work, Ms. Dunn said. She said lots of things like that.

I qualified in the eight hundred and in the long jump for the state meet in Framingham. It was on the first Saturday in August. I was hoping Mom would come home for it. She'd come home every time Scott pitched in the Babe Ruth league. But the night before the meet, she called from the shop to wish me luck.

"Not that you'll need it," she said. "Dad tells me you're a regular comet."

"A lot of the kids are older," I said. "Maybe I won't be fast at all."

Mom was quiet for a minute. I could hear the bell on the shop door jingle in the background. Then she said, "I would come, Tessa, but you know how impossible weekend traffic is. Just try to have a good race, and call me when you get home."

Dad and I rode to Framingham in the Arvids' van with Trudy and her parents and her brother. Rob made me think about Scott, and I didn't want to. Scott wouldn't have gone to my race either.

My first long jump was the farthest of everybody, but my foot touched the line, so it didn't count. My other two jumps were okay. I got second place. Sammy Collins from Wardsboro got third. Ms. Dunn was real excited.

I was nervous about the eight hundred. There were enough kids running it to have three separate races. I ran in the first one.

"How're you doing?" Ms. Dunn asked when I was getting ready.

I tied my laces in double knots. "I don't feel so good," I said. "It's different here."

Ms. Dunn refastened my barrettes. "It is very different," she said. "But you're the same Tessa. If you can remember why you run, I think you'll be just fine."

I guess she could tell I didn't have any idea right then why I was running. "Do you run because you want to win or because you like to run?" she asked.

I thought about it. "I like to win," I said. Then I remembered how it felt when I was running and I said, "But I would run even if I never won anything."

Ms. Dunn hugged me. "You pay attention to that and you'll be just fine, no matter what."

And I was. The girl next to me was ahead on the first lap. When I tried to go faster I felt all jumbled, so I just stopped looking at her. I slowed down until my hair and my arms and legs and breathing all matched up. I began to feel strong and happy. I didn't hear anybody, not even Dad. When I crossed the finish line, the girl who was ahead wasn't anymore. After the other races were run, my time was best.

Trudy came in third for the fifteen hundred, which was very good. We all ate at Friendly's on the way home. We had milkshakes and all the parents toasted our team. Then the team toasted Ms. Dunn for being such a good coach.

I called Mom when we got home. I liked telling her I won. But I liked even better how I felt inside, and that had nothing to do with winning. There was a place in me that fit together whether outside did or not.

I COULD HAVE RUN at Regionals in Hershey, Pennsylvania, but I didn't want to. Ms. Dunn couldn't go, and it was Dad's vacation. We were going to Truro for a week, then I was going to stay there while Dad went to Boston to paint Gramma and Grampa's house.

The Wednesday before I went, Bubbe took Hannah and me to Larkspur and Lovage for tea. There were tables with umbrellas outdoors in their flower gardens. Each table was in a different flower garden. You got to choose which flowers you wanted to eat with.

We chose hollyhocks, delphiniums, and purple coneflowers. We had scones and jam with whipped cream, and little cucumber sandwiches. Hannah and I had lemonade, and Bubbe had blackberry tea. We went in a taxi.

"Will your mother come home after your vacation?" Hannah asked. She was going to Lake Winnipesaukee in New Hampshire the same time I was going to Truro.

"Maybe," I said. "The shop won't be so busy when school starts."

"She will come, *bubeleh*," Bubbe said. "And not because the shop does not need her. I know it in here." She thumped her chest with her fist.

When Bubbe said that and thumped her chest, she was almost always right. There were four big strawberries in the middle of the scone plate. "Two strawberries are for you, Bubbe," I said.

It was ninety-five degrees hot on Friday. Mrs. Goldberg called from her office to tell me to drink a big glass of water before I started on my paper route. Hannah said even her eyeballs were sweating. She didn't want to go to her piano lesson, but Mrs. Goldberg told her to go anyway.

Hal opened the freezer case when I came in. "Take your pick, young lady." I chose a grape Popsicle. "You put your running legs to good use today," he said as he helped me load my bag. "Those clouds look serious."

I went as fast as I could. The air felt like our bathroom does after somebody's taken a hot shower. Heat lightning flickered in the sky beyond Boylston Street.

"I'm going to Truro for two weeks," I told Mr. Doyle. "Adam Kestler will deliver the paper."

"Have a good time and find me a sand dollar," he said. "Now get a wiggle on. I can smell that storm coming."

On Chestnut Street I stopped to hug and kiss Bubbe good-bye, then I ran. One minute it was so quiet all I could hear was my own breathing. The next minute trees were thrashing, and trash cans and lawn chairs banged about. I was at the other end of Pine Street from Hannah's house when the rain hit. It came so hard I was soaked in a second.

A car stopped at the curb, and the passenger door

opened. "Get in!" yelled Ms. Dunn. Lightning flared as I pulled the door shut.

"That was a bit of luck!" Ms. Dunn said. "I was driving up Boylston when I saw you round the corner. That sky is black as night!" She reached in back for a beach towel and wrapped it around me. Thunder and lightning were going like the Fourth of July. "We're as safe here as anywhere. Are you afraid of thunderstorms, Tessa?"

I shook my head. "Not if I'm inside," I said. "I like to watch them."

"Me, too." Ms. Dunn rubbed the fog off the inside of the windshield. "My brother was afraid of them. He'd walk the ridgepole at my grandfather's farm, he'd dive from the highest rock at the river, but he was afraid of thunderstorms."

"I didn't know you had a brother," I said. I didn't know anything about Ms. Dunn except for school and track.

"Yes," she said. "I did. I've wanted to tell you about him, but there's never been the time or the place. And some people would say it's not professional to share your personal life with your students."

I rubbed my hair with the towel and waited. It was

raining so hard it was like going through the car wash. Inside the car felt safe and secret.

Ms. Dunn settled sideways in her seat. "There were five children in my family," she began. "First was my brother, all by himself for four years, then me. The others came later. My mother thought no one was smarter, no one more handsome, than her boy. My father never referred to him as Tommy. He called him 'My Son.' And when I came along, well, I adored him, too."

Ms. Dunn smiled. "He, of course, in all his glory, took little notice of me. So I would do things to annoy him, just to get his attention."

"Like what?" I asked.

"Oh, when I was real little, my mother said I would try to hold on to his shirt whenever he went out. I followed him everywhere. Some older brothers and sisters don't mind that, but he sure did. Later I spied on him. I would threaten to tell what I knew if he didn't play with me."

"I tried that once," I said. "It didn't work. I think Scott knew I wouldn't tell anyway."

Ms. Dunn laughed. "As I got older, about the only thing my brother and I did together was fight," she said. "But when I won the violin competition, when I got a gold star for spelling, he was the one I told first. And at Christmas, I spent more on his gift than on anyone else's."

I cleared my throat. "Last Christmas I got Scott a harmonica CD he wanted. I only had nine dollars left for Mom and Dad. I got him a key ring with his name on it for his birthday. He never got to use the key ring."

"I bet he liked it, though," Ms. Dunn said.

I nodded. "He was going to get his license in the spring."

The rain roared on the car, quieted, then roared again.

"The winter I was nine years old, my brother was thirteen." I had to listen hard to hear Ms. Dunn's voice. "There was a river where we lived. It came in from the sea. If it got cold enough, the river would freeze. Because of the tide, the ice was in chunks. 'Stay away from the river, keep off the ice.' Every kid in town was taught that before anything else."

Ms. Dunn looked at me. "Of course, some kids didn't stay off the ice. It was a game. They would jump from chunk to chunk to see who could get across the river the fastest. My brother was one of the best. I would beg him not to do it, but he did."

Ms. Dunn straightened and rubbed at the window again. "One day he slipped. Right off the ice, down between the chunks. Just like that. No one saw him again."

I looked straight ahead. "Were you there?"

Ms. Dunn sighed big. "No, thank God, I didn't see it happen. Not for real. But in my head I saw it. I still do."

"Did you tell your parents you knew he went on the ice?"

Ms. Dunn shook her head. "No," she said. "Nobody talked about it after, and I didn't either. My mother stopped smiling, and my father started drinking, but nobody talked. The priest at our church tried to help. One day he brought me a blue notebook. He said sometimes it helped to write things down."

The rain had slowed enough so Ms. Dunn could open the windows a little. "That is what I wanted to tell you, Tessa. In case it might help you the way it did me. I began a Tommy book. I put in the good things, I put in the bad things. Every single thing I could remember."

"The bad things, too?" I said.

"Oh, yes. Tommy could be very mean sometimes. I had to stay three lampposts behind him when we walked to school. He called me names you wouldn't believe. He threw stones at my Anna doll for target practice."

"Scott called me Puke Head and Butt Wipe," I said. "He wouldn't let me in his room. Once when he was gone, I went in and wrote *Scott Snot* all over everything. He made me erase it, but you could still see."

Ms. Dunn laughed so hard she cried. "Oh, we go on, Tessa," she said. "We go on."

And suddenly I told her. "I knew Scott was going with Kevin Olsen the night he died. He wasn't supposed to ride with him, but I didn't tell."

"Of course you didn't." Ms. Dunn was serious again. "Do you think it would have made a difference if you did?"

I had thought about that. A lot. "Maybe not," I said. "He would have said it wasn't true. My mother always believed him. They were kindred spirits."

"But it still bothers you," Ms. Dunn said. "Because you can't know for sure."

I nodded.

"All I know, Tessa, is that Scott's death wasn't your fault, just as Tommy's wasn't mine. Write about it, sweetheart. Maybe it will help."

The storm went as fast as it came. I said good-bye to Ms. Dunn and finished my route. When I got to Maple Street, Clementine came out from under her porch and chased my shoelaces all the way to WomenCenter.

Mrs. Goldberg was just finishing up. "I was worried about you, Tessa," she said. "I would have left my client and looked for you if I had the car."

"Ms. Dunn saw me," I said. "We sat in her car and talked."

"I hoped you'd find shelter someplace. Are you all packed for Truro?"

"Not yet." I hopped next to her along the sidewalk, one foot in each square. "I'll get ready tonight. Can I go to Fishman's? I need to get a notebook."

"I'll go with you," Mrs. Goldberg said. "I need a few things, too. What are you going to do with a notebook?"

"I'm going to write a book," I said. "I'm going to write about my brother."

SATURDAY NIGHT, the first night we were in Truro, I dreamed I was in a field. The grass came up to my waist and went as far as I could see. When I pushed it away, I could see gravestones flat on the ground. I was looking for Scott's. I knew it might take a very long time to find it in that huge field, but I kept looking. The stones were only here and there. I could feel them with my feet. After looking and looking, I saw the letters OND on one. I knelt down to look more closely. The stone said THERESA GRACE DRUMMOND. The date was February 17.

That was the day Scott was killed. But it wasn't his name on the stone. It was mine.

I woke up after that. I felt like I did the time I fell flat on my stomach in the race and couldn't catch my breath. When I woke again, it was morning. I felt tired from looking for that stone all night and strange about my name being on it.

"You're a quiet puss," Aunt Rhoda said when she and I were eating cereal out on the patio. "What would you like to do this morning?"

"Where are my parents?" I was cold even in the sun.

"I don't know, sweetie. They rode off on the bikes just before you came down."

"Let's go to Fort Hill, then," I said. That was way down in Eastham. If we walked around the longest trail there, we wouldn't get back until it was time for Aunt Rhoda to go to work. Her shop opened late on Sundays.

"Don't you want to go there with your parents?" Aunt Rhoda looked at me over the top of her glasses. She was wearing lime-green ones.

"They can go by themselves another time," I said. I wanted my parents to be alone as much as possible.

A magazine I read at WomenCenter said it was important for married people to have time to themselves. It said they should go on dates like before they were married.

We walked the trails at Fort Hill every year. Scott and I used to climb the trees in Cedar Swamp. We have a picture of Scott sitting on a huge branch like it was a horse. He was holding me in front of him.

This year I was interested when Aunt Rhoda pointed out across the salt marsh to where Henry David Thoreau used to have his cabin. Mr. Gomez loved Henry David Thoreau. He said one of the reasons he came to teach in Wardsboro was because it wasn't far from where Thoreau lived. He took us on a field trip to Walden Pond, and he was always saying things that Thoreau wrote.

We stopped at PJ's and had lobster rolls on the way back. "You're looking better than you did when you were here for the Fourth of July," Aunt Rhoda said. "I guess you and your dad have been doing all right?"

I sucked the last of my chocolate milkshake from around the bottom of my cup and nodded.

"Tessa, look at me." Aunt Rhoda reached across the

table and put her hand over mine. "I know that you and your dad need your mother. And she needs you, whether she knows it or not. She's let her grief over Scott close her eyes to everyone else. I could just SHAKE her!"

I stared at Aunt Rhoda. "Do you mean she's not coming back with us ever?"

"No! No, sweetie, that's not what I'm saying!" Aunt Rhoda squeezed my hand. "I just want you to understand that in grieving, people can do and say things they never would otherwise. The other day your mother told me that because I didn't have children I couldn't possibly know what she was going through. As though I didn't have four straight miscarriages when I was married to that creep Albert. Another time when a customer in the shop complained about the rain, Shirley told her very sharply to count her blessings. My little sister, who apologizes to a plant if she's five minutes late watering it."

I wished I hadn't sucked down the milkshake so fast. It was giving me a stomachache. "Will she stop being different?" I asked.

Aunt Rhoda nodded vigorously. "For sure," she said. "Don't you worry, Tessa. It's going to be all right." She checked her teeth in her compact mirror, then started collecting our stuff. "Come on. My shop awaits. We hired two more girls, but we're still shorthanded."

Every morning that week I took my notebook and went across the field to sit under the apple tree that huddled behind the dunes. That was my special place. I kept a perfect wishing rock I found on the beach in a hole in the trunk. Even on very hot days the stone was cool and smooth in my hand.

I'd bought a green notebook at Fishman's because that was Scott's favorite color. I thought maybe I should start at the beginning of what I remembered, so I wrote first about Scott holding me on the tree in Cedar Swamp. I wasn't sure if I really remembered him doing that or if I just remembered the picture, but I liked thinking about it, so I put it in.

Because of talking to Ms. Dunn, I made a list of all the presents I could remember ever giving Scott. I gave him a Red Sox magnet, a pencil shaped like a baseball bat, a Calvin and Hobbes snow globe because that was his favorite comic strip, twenty-five packs of baseball cards, some socks with maroon and gold stripes because those were Wardsboro High colors.

I gave him a bag of caramels once. He didn't let me have a single one, even though he had braces at the time and wasn't supposed to eat caramels.

I also made a list of the things Scott gave me. When I was in first grade, he gave me a purple velvet headband. Purple was my favorite color. I wore the headband to school and felt it soft and purple in my hair all day. When it was time to go home, I reached up and it was gone. I sat on the school steps after everybody left. I couldn't go home without it. My teacher saw me there and helped me look everywhere I'd been inside the school. Then we looked out on the playground. We found my headband under the jungle gym. The velvet was squashed and the purple all dusty. It wasn't the same at all. I didn't want it anymore. It still made me feel sad to think about it. That and the birthstone ring he gave me when I was eight were my favorite presents from Scott. The ring was too small now. It was in my tea can at home with my baby teeth.

I figured while I was writing in my book, Mom and Dad were spending time together. In the afternoons we usually went to the beach. Dad fished and Mom read and I played in the waves and looked for

Mr. Doyle's sand dollar. Mom didn't go to work until after supper the whole time Dad was there. The night we took a picnic to the bay and watched the sunset, she didn't go to the shop at all.

Dad left on the second Monday to go paint Gramma and Grampa's house. Mom wasn't too happy about his going, which I thought was a good sign.

"Why don't they just hire someone, Ed?" Mom asked at breakfast. "It's not as though they don't have the money."

"They have it," Dad agreed. "But they don't want to spend it. I don't mind. I haven't done much for them these past months. If this weather holds, I should be back by Friday. We can head home anytime after that."

"Sunday morning," Mom said, just like that. "I'll finish up at Rhoda's Saturday night. We'll go first thing so you'll have time to settle before starting back to work Monday."

I looked up and met Dad's eyes. The way he smiled I could tell he hadn't been sure either that Mom would be coming with us.

"Sounds good to me." Dad cleared the table, then went to get his duffel. He was still smiling when he backed out through the hedge. I ran out to the road and waved until he went around the curve behind the scrub pine. I watched for his car on the far hill. When I turned to go back to the house, Mom was right behind me.

"You'll miss him, won't you?" she said, and I nodded. "I had no doubt the two of you would be just fine this summer." She stood with her hands on her hips and looked at the hedge. "I'd better trim this before I go. Rhoda won't do it, she likes it wild." Mom went off to get the hedge clippers. When she came back, she started working at the far end from where I was standing.

"I guess I'll look for shells," I called. She nodded without looking up. "Be back by noon," she said. "I'm working afternoons this week to finish up."

I put my Scott book in the bag I collect shells in and started off across the field. I threw the bag under the apple tree and kept going up over the dune. I slid down the other side and just sat there. Why didn't Mom want to come to the beach with me? I'd been happy about her coming home with us, and now I felt all sad and lonely.

I got up and ran across the beach to the hard-packed sand at the edge of the tide. I ran as far and as fast as I could, then I sat until the waves swirled up around me.

It was a long way back to the path over the dunes. I sat under the apple tree in a spot where the sun came through the branches, and opened my book.

I hate Scott, I wrote. *He was a liar. He lied to Mom about going with Kevin. He lied to Mom about drinking. He was a stupid selfish pig. He was mean. He was mean to leave Grady for Kevin. He was mean to me. All the time. He went over to Grady's last summer when he was supposed to stay with me while Mom and Dad went to a play and there was a thunderstorm and I didn't tell. Rob Arvid took Trudy to see the Boston Marathon. He took her to the French circus. He went to her race and he cheered and cheered. Scott never took me anywhere. He didn't like me. He didn't even notice me. If I died he wouldn't think of one single thing to write about me in a book. He called me Amazon Annie because I'm good at sports. Mom said he loved me but she didn't know. Mom loved Scott more than anybody. He was her favorite person in the whole world. I HATE SCOTT HE IS DEAD.*

I sat for a long time, doing nothing. The edge of my shorts was stiff with salt where they dried in the sun. A grasshopper landed on top of what I had written. When it jumped off, I turned to a new page.

Last summer after the game where Scott got a hit that scored a run he bought me a Fudgsicle. Sometimes he let Hannah and me play with the scrimshaw chess set he got from Pops. Sometimes in Truro we did jigsaw puzzles when it rained. I wish Scott was here now. I wish Mom wanted to be with me too.

I closed the book. I couldn't think of anything else to write.

THE REST OF THE WEEK I helped in the store and I played on the beach. I found two perfect sand dollars. I kept one for Mr. Doyle and put the other in the hole in the apple tree. I read two mysteries, and on Thursday I went deep-sea fishing with Angel Cardova. I caught a bluefish. We ate it for dinner that night and then had the rest for chowder when Dad came. Sunday morning we packed up and went home to Wardsboro, just like Mom said.

I was behind her when she went upstairs for the first time. She stopped at Scott's door, then went on down the hall to her own room. I thought it was a good sign she left his door open. I opened my windows and unpacked my things and was starting downstairs to call Hannah when I heard my mother say, "I guess I loved him too much." I could tell she was crying.

I knew you weren't supposed to listen when people didn't know you were doing it, but my legs wouldn't work. I sat down fast on the stairs, and I didn't cover my ears.

Dad said, "I don't think we can ever love too much, Shirley, only too little."

"What are you saying, Ed? That I didn't love Scott enough? He was the light of my life! He was—"

"That's not what I'm saying at all."

"What then? That I don't love you or Tessa enough? That I'm failing you? Where do I get the strength to do anything else? I'm the one drowning here. You and Tessa are doing just fine. Right from the start, the both of you went off to work and school like you were escaping from some prison. I can't just continue on like nothing happened. I don't go five minutes without seeing Scott, hearing Scott, yearning for Scott. . . ."

"Which maybe is why you don't see or hear Tessa.

She needs you, Shirley. Have you wondered what she's writing in that book she went off with every morning? She held it on her lap the whole way home."

My legs worked fine now. I was down the stairs and out the door, heading for Chestnut Street.

Bubbe was reading on her porch. She saw me from three houses away.

"*There's* my *bubeleh,*" she called, as though she'd been waiting for me. "You come up here now, we have a visit."

I sat in the green rocker next to hers. She reached over and patted my hand. "You tell me," she said when I'd got my breath. "You tell me, Tessa."

"My mother came back," I said. "But maybe she won't stay."

"When she come, Tessa?"

"Today," I said. "We just got back."

"Give her time, Tessa, give her time! Right now all she see are reminders."

"She was yelling. She thinks my father and I don't care as much. She loved Scott best."

Bubbe was still patting my hand. "Of course. We always love best the one who die. To love them is easy. To love ones right here is harder. That take . . ."

Bubbe made great rolling circles with her arms. "What is the word?"

"Energy?" I guessed, watching her arms churn.

"You see? You hear my heart. We are . . ." Bubbe clasped her hands on her chest.

"What if she doesn't get energy?" I asked.

"A girl like you and a man like your papa? She get her energy, *bubeleh*. Oh yes. You give her time."

I wasn't so sure. It had already been a long time. I was glad to hear it was still a possibility, though. "Maybe if I help a lot," I said.

But Bubbe shook her head. "Helping is good, we all help. But you don't make the sad, *bubeleh*. You can't fix what happen. Your mama love you. You help her by remembering that."

I rocked and thought about it. Bubbe was right. It seemed like a very long time since Scott died, but it was only half a year. Of course my mother loved me. She loved my dad, too. She just couldn't pay attention to it because of feeling so bad about Scott.

As soon as Dad left for work Monday morning, Mom called Worthington Bank and Fairfield Accounting to tell them she was ready for any work they had for her. I guess they had a lot. When Hannah and I came back from the library that afternoon, she was working in her office. She was either there or in meetings the rest of the week.

It was the last week before school started. One night we went to Tastee-Freez after supper. Another night we went to the last band concert of the summer in the park with the Goldbergs. My parents cooked supper together and talked more than before Mom went away, but I didn't see any kissing. Mr. and Mrs. Goldberg kissed a lot, but Brittany Bevins told me once her parents never kissed. They weren't divorced, either, like Emma Washburn's parents.

After my paper route on Friday, Mom took me shopping for school clothes. She hates malls, so we walked downtown to Youngsters. It was the first time Mom let me pick out everything. She even let me get purple high-top sneakers.

"The rate you're growing we'll be lucky these things last you till Christmas," Mom said when we were walking home. "You're tall like your dad."

"You and Aunt Rhoda are tall, too," I said.

"Oh, I was a little thing when I was a kid," Mom said. "My mother used to make me take cod-liver oil.

I was like Scott. I didn't begin to grow until I was in high school."

"My corduroys still fit," I said.

"Not for long," Mom said. "They're getting pretty high-water."

"Adam Kestler is taller than I am," I said. "And so is Trudy Arvid." Which wasn't true. Trudy and I were the same height.

Mom looked at me. "Tessa, you're fine! It's good to be tall and healthy!"

But right then I wished I was tiny and had asthma.

HANNAH AND I WORE SHIRTS I'd brought back from Aunt Rhoda's shop for the first day of school. Mine had a picture of a humpback whale on it and Hannah's had a finback. I'd found a postcard of Thoreau's cottage in Provincetown for Mr. Gomez. It said: *Dreams are the touchstones of our characters.* I figured he'd know what it meant.

Brittany Bevins was waiting for us on the front steps. "Guess what!" she called when we were still down the walk. She had her annoying little smile that means she knows something you don't. "You'll never believe it!"

"Probably not," Hannah said.

"You're going to die, Tessa. You're really going to *die!* Of course, I liked her, too, but—"

"Say it or shut up." I stared at her, but her smile just got bigger.

"Miss . . . Dunn . . . isn't . . . coming . . . back!"

I didn't give her one bit of satisfaction. "So?" I said, and went on by to the door.

"Don't you want to know why?"

Hannah stayed with Brittany to hear, but I kept going. I didn't believe it. Ms. Dunn would have told me if she wasn't coming back. Brittany Bevins didn't know a single thing about her.

Hannah caught up to me in the coatroom. "She said at the last minute Ms. Dunn's contract wasn't renewed. She said that only happens when there's something really serious."

"Like what?" I asked.

"Like maybe shoplifting. That's what Brittany thinks it is."

"That's not true," I said. "Ms. Dunn would never do that. You know Brittany likes to say mean things. She's a puke head."

But everybody was talking about it. Someone besides Brittany said Ms. Dunn had been caught walking out of WriteWell Stationers with a pocket calculator and some rollerball pens. Other kids said people had complained about her teaching methods to the school board. Walter Plum said they couldn't legally fire her unless they could prove she was unfit. He said it probably was a morals case. Adam Kestler said shut up, Walter, you don't know what you're talking about. He said anyone with half a brain knew Ms. Dunn was the fittest teacher on the planet. When he said that, I liked Adam Kestler even more than I did before.

I didn't believe any of it until we went to music after lunch. Ms. Dunn wasn't waiting at the door to swish us through with one of her scarves. No music was playing. The mobiles still hung from the ceiling, but the masks from Mexico were gone. It was just an ordinary room, with an ordinary teacher telling us to sit down. She said her name was Mrs. Burbank and that she was trained in the Orff method of teaching music.

"Since this is a music class," she said, "I think it appropriate that we start our journey together with a song. Now then, who can suggest something we're all sure to know?"

Walter Plum raised his hand. "'Row, Row, Row Your Boat'?"

"Yes! Excellent!" Mrs. Burbank couldn't tell Walter was being a wiseacre. She divided us into sections and directed us as if we were the Boston Symphony. She didn't do it for fun, either, like Ms. Dunn sometimes did. Then she used that stupid song to show us the Orff system of ta-tays and ta-fa-tiffys. With Ms. Dunn we'd compared musical patterns of composers like Beethoven and Mozart to pop songs we liked. Nobody sang "Row, Row, Row Your Boat" unless they were five years old or on a long, boring trip in the car.

By the end of school, I felt really sick. I ran all the way home and up to my room. When Hannah called, I pretended I was sleeping. I didn't want to go to music ever again. My head hurt, and it was hard to breathe right. Maybe I was allergic to something in the music room and could get excused. Emma Washburn got out of gym because of being allergic to some kind of mold.

I heard Dad come home, but I didn't want any supper. I couldn't stop shivering. I found some winter pajamas and got under the covers. Mom came up and felt my head. "You don't have a fever, Tessa. You feel cold as ice. Did you eat something bad?"

I shook my head. It hurt to move it. "I'm just tired," I said.

I heard Dad talking on the phone, then his feet on the stairs. He came in and sat on the edge of my bed. I kept my eyes shut. He took my hand and traced around each finger. His hand felt nice and warm. After a while he said quietly, "Is this about Ms. Dunn?"

I turned away from him.

"Because I just talked to Jane Goldberg. She said Ms. Dunn has resigned."

I swallowed, and managed to whisper, "I don't care."

I felt my bed go down on the other side. Mom said, "You must care very much. She was a fine teacher, and she was your friend."

"She *wasn't* my friend." I shot up between them. "Friends don't just leave without telling you. She didn't care about me at *all*. I *hate* her." My voice had risen until I was screaming right at Mom. "I *hate* her."

Dad started to say something, but Mom put out her hand to stop him. She reached her arms around me and pulled me close against her. "There, there," she whispered. "It's okay, Tessa. It's okay."

She held me for a long time, rocking me back and forth. I would think I was all done crying, then I would start up again. Dad got a box of tissues, and we sat there together like we could stay forever if I wanted.

After a while Mom said, "Tell me about her, Tessa. Tell me why she was so special."

I could see Ms. Dunn, smiling at me the way she always did. "She was tall as you, Mom. And she had long curly hair like yours, only red, and she had really green eyes. Some days she was kind of quiet and looked sad, but mostly not. I always liked being near her. I liked her room and the music and how I felt. She knew just what to say, like she could see inside you. She always wore a little silver pin of a bird flying. Sometimes it was on her pocket or her headband or her sleeve. Once I looked and looked. It was on the cuff of her pants. She was nice to everybody, even Brittany Bevins, but she made me feel like I was special. I think she made most kids feel like that."

"Like my Miss Reid," Mom said. "She lived next door to us when I was little. If I was mad at Rhoda, or in trouble with my parents, I could go to her. She liked my whole family, but I did feel I was special."

"What happened to her?" I asked.

"We moved away when I was twelve," Mom said. "She died a few years after that. But I still think about her, and I still feel special when I do."

I blew my nose. "How could Ms. Dunn go without telling me?"

"You've been in Truro," Mom said. "Maybe she didn't have a chance, or know how. Maybe she will. We don't know what really happened. People we love aren't perfect, Tessa. None of us ever are."

"She wouldn't steal," I said. "She wouldn't do anything bad."

"Probably not." Mom stroked my hair. "But whatever did or didn't happen doesn't change what you know and love about Ms. Dunn."

I thought it over, and I knew it was true.

"I need her," I whispered.

Mom pulled me close again. "I know you do, Tessa. I'll try so you don't need her quite so much."

Mom and Dad tucked the covers around me then and kissed me good night. Just before my eyes closed, I saw them standing in the doorway with their arms around each other.

I DIDN'T HAVE TO GO to music class and do ta-tays with Mrs. Burbank because Mom arranged for me to take band instead. I chose the oboe. It was hard, but I liked it. I went to Wardsboro Conservatory for lessons on Wednesday afternoons.

We still didn't know for sure what happened with Ms. Dunn. The school board said they couldn't comment on personnel matters. Mrs. Goldberg said the Wardsboro school board made things difficult for teachers with new ideas. She was going to run for the board in the spring.

Mom and Dad started going to grief counseling in

October. They went on Monday nights while I stayed at the Goldbergs. I liked how my parents talked late after we got home and I'd gone to bed. Sometimes Mom cried, but it didn't scare me like before. I was pretty sure now she wasn't going to leave us.

One warm afternoon in November, Mom and Mrs. Goldberg were sitting on the Goldbergs' front steps, drinking tea and talking. Hannah and I were raking leaves into huge piles. I was lying in one of them when I heard Mom say, "I'm beginning to understand that real loving isn't threatened by truths that don't suit us. It doesn't ask us to look the other way."

I was still thinking about what she said when we were walking home. We were almost to our corner when Mom said, "You're awfully quiet. Is something bothering you?"

I nodded yes, then shook my head no. I wanted to tell her, but I couldn't. What if it made things bad again?

Mom stopped and took both my hands. "What is it, Tessa?"

An ant was dragging a little crumb along the sidewalk. I watched until it disappeared into a crack.

"I knew," I whispered.

Mom bent down. "What? You knew?"

I nodded.

Mom put her cheek against mine. "What did you know?" she asked gently.

"I knew Scott was going with Kevin that night."

I had said it. I had told my mother.

She didn't seem awfully upset. She kept her cheek against mine and murmured, "Oh, sweetheart! Oh, Tessa."

She straightened up and looked at me. "You've been keeping this to yourself all this time? Why didn't you say something?"

"I didn't want to tell on him," I said. "I didn't want him to be mad at me."

"Of course you didn't," Mom said. "I understand that. I have a big sister."

"But then he got killed," I said. "If I'd told, maybe he wouldn't have." I started to cry.

"Oh no, Tessa!" Mom said. "No, no, no! Scott would have talked his way out of it. I wanted to believe him more than I wanted to know the truth. That's what I was just saying to Jane. Besides, it was Dad's and my job to know what Scott was doing, not yours. And it was his responsibility, too. Oh, Tessa, *none* of this was your fault."

Mom was wiping my eyes and holding the tissue for me to blow my nose the way she did when I was little. "Tell me you believe that, Tessa. Tell me you understand."

I nodded. "Okay," I said. I smiled at her. "I'm okay."

And I was. I knew Ms. Dunn didn't think Scott's dying was my fault. I figured Dad wouldn't think so either. But until that afternoon, I hadn't been sure about Mom.

"Except for getting old," Bubbe told me, "most things in life go two steps forward, one step back." It was December 5, the day before Scott's birthday. Lots of houses on my paper route were already decorated with Christmas lights.

"Everybody, all over the world, they light up the darkest days," Bubbe said. "It is very brave, I think, *bubeleh*. It is hope. You put lights on a tree, I put candles in my menorah. We all make light in the dark time."

"I'm not sure we will this year," I said. "Mom's quiet again because of Scott's birthday. Even going to counseling didn't help."

That's when Bubbe said we go two steps forward, one step back. "Especially with such sorrow," she said. "We learn to go on, but days come, maybe years after, we think we forget how."

Dad spent the next morning in his workshop. He wasn't making anything, he was just sorting pieces of wood and cleaning his tools. "You got plans today?" he asked when I came to sit on the stairs and watch.

I shook my head. "No."

"It's a day to be got through," Dad said. "When Mom gets done talking to Rhoda on the phone, I'm thinking of heading out. Maybe we'll drive up to Plum Island, walk along the water a bit, find a nice place for lunch. How about it?"

"Can I stay here? If it's okay with Mrs. Goldberg and Hannah comes over?" Because if my parents were going someplace, I had a plan.

As soon as Mom and Dad left, I went upstairs and got my tea can out of my underwear drawer. The ring Scott gave me didn't fit even my little finger now. I put it on the chain from a locket Gramma and Grampa Drummond gave me, and fastened it around my neck.

Hannah came over and we made peanut-butter-

and-banana sandwiches. Then we went up to the attic and got out the Christmas lights.

"Is it okay with your parents?" Hannah asked when we were untangling the strings. "Won't they want to help?"

"It's a surprise," I said. "We usually wait until after Scott's birthday. But this year we need the lights now."

It took us a long time. We had to find extension cords, and then we had to go to Fishman's to get some new bulbs. We put the candles in the windows. We put the little white lights all over the bushes out front. Everything was ready by the time it started getting dark.

Hannah and I were outside on the sidewalk looking at how pretty it was when my parents got back. The car stopped before it turned into the driveway. For just a second I was afraid I'd made a big mistake. Then Dad rolled down his window, and I could tell it was okay.

They came to stand on the sidewalk with us. Mom had tears in her eyes. "It's just the right thing, Tessa," she whispered. "How did you know?"

"Bubbe said it's important to put lights in the darkness. That's when they shine best."

"They certainly do." Mom put one arm around me and the other around Hannah. "Let's call your folks, Hannah, and see if they'd like to come enjoy your handiwork. We could order some pizza."

GRADY ALLEN CAME for a little while Christmas Eve, just like he always did. The doorbell rang, and there he was. Mom hugged him to pieces, and so did Dad. Grady didn't seem to mind. Mom said it was her best Christmas present.

My best present was a picture Mrs. Goldberg gave me the first night of Hanukkah. It was Ms. Dunn and me at a track meet. Ms. Dunn's hands were on my shoulders and we were looking at each other. Mrs. Goldberg put it in a wooden frame she got at Picture Perfect. The next day Mom took me there so I could buy a frame just like it for the picture of Scott and me in the Cedar Swamp tree. I put them on the table next to my bed.

Aunt Rhoda stayed with us the week after Christmas. On New Year's Eve, Mom and Dad invited Bubbe and the Goldbergs to dinner. Dad made poached salmon, Mom made broccoli soufflé, Aunt Rhoda made five-spice rice, and Hannah and I made brownie sundaes. Before we ate, Mom raised her glass to toast the Goldbergs and Bubbe. "Thank you," she said. "Yes," Dad said. Aunt Rhoda said, "Here, here!"

After everybody left, I was lying on the couch with my head in Mom's lap and my legs in Dad's. Mom was watching the fire and playing with my hair. Dad was reading us a story by Wendell Berry.

Aunt Rhoda was half asleep in the recliner. "I don't think I'm going to make it," she said when Dad finished. She was supposed to meet a friend at ten o'clock and go dancing.

"Rhoda," Mom said. Her voice was wide-awake. "Look at that."

"What?" Aunt Rhoda was still staring at the fire.

"Look at Tessa's hand."

Aunt Rhoda yawned. "What about it?"

"The way she's holding it. I never noticed before. It's the way I hold mine, the way Aunt Dell and Dad held theirs. All curled up with the thumb between the last two fingers."

Everybody looked at my hand. "Well, what do you know," Aunt Rhoda said. "The mark of a true Andrews. I used to try to hold mine that way when I remembered."

Dad winked at me. "The hand may be Andrews, but I still claim the eyes."

"Yes," said Mom. She smiled at him. "Those beautiful eyes, and the Andrews hand. She's our girl, all right."